LEADERS

AND

LEGENDS

LEADERS AND LEGENDS

DON GIOVANNI PR

Title: Leaders and Legends

Author: Don Giovanni PR

No part of this publication may be reproduced, stored in a retrieval system, or transmitted by any means: electronic, mechanical, photocopy, recording, scanning, or otherwise, except as permitted under section 107 or 108 of the 1976 United States Act, without the prior written permission of the author.

First Edition

DG Prom

Dover, Delaware

Dedication

Leaders and Legends is dedicated to those remarkable characters - past and present – whose wisdom, craft, strength, passion, and determination, have been a great contribution to the development of man's civilization. The first poem is dedicated to the greatest leader – God. The last poem is dedicated to a mythological figure - Narcissus.

CONTENTS

ACKNOWLEDGMENTS

Many thanks to my Creator for my life, and for the opportunity to write and share these verses.

Thanks to my mother and my maternal grandmother for their great love, their guidance, and their support. Thanks to my daughter Lorna whose love and caring have been instrumental during the past few years. Thanks to my son, Giovanni and my daughters Laura, Felicita, and Sandra Marie; my sister Carmen Iris, and my present love, Luz Nereida (Princesa) - for sharing a brief interval of happiness in my life and for being an inspirational source.

POEMS

GOD

An invisible force to human eyes,

The greatest power ever known,

Reaching beyond the stars and life,

Infinity Himself, is our mighty God.

He's the Creator of existence and mankind,

The Giver, the Protector of the smallest form,

The Eternal Light that that breaks the night

Overwhelming the darkness of the unknown.

Behold Him In your dreams and minds,

Treasure his kindness and eternal love,

Detach yourselves from pettiness that binds

And surrender to Him your souls and hopes.

STARS

(Inspired by expressions of Dr. Kaku)

Blazing through space and time

And the forbidden corridors of emptiness,

The Masters of the Universe – the STARS -

Burn through their life and death.

Queens of the Cosmic Stage,

Stars challenge the darkness of the void

Crushing the shadows on their way,

Seeding with life the universal soil.

Behold the greatest moment, humankind!

Of the cosmic existence of the Stars,

For they will fade into the eternal night

As they return to the Creator's hands.

Woman

Loveliest of creatures ever born
In the reckless arena of Mother Earth,
You march along the jungle road
Guarding an ever-growing human race.

Beyond the dawn of man you move ahead,
Rising from social prejudice and bonds
To level-off with the king of the world
And share the power of the conqueror.

You're strong, dedicated, and smart,
A companion whose passion never stops,
Sharing the deepest feelings of your heart
To lead us thru the road of peace and love.

President George Washington

(First President)

Leader and father of a growing nation

Whose great concern and military skills

Brought him to work on the foundation

Of the land to become Home of the Free.

Ingenious strategist, well disciplined, and above all,

A leader who set on fire the rebellious hearts

To challenge and defeat the powerful imperial forces

That ruled and controlled their colonial way of life.

General and commander of the continental troops,

And later, first President of the United States,

George Washington, a symbol of honor and truth,

Became the founder of the greatest nation in the world.

President Ronald Reagan

(Peace Maker)

He turned the world of politics around

And set us free from the rumors of war,

Bringing to-an end- the silent count

Of the Cold War threating humankind.

A peace maker, a leader, a family man.

Reagan was a defender of the human rights,

A lovely father, a loving and beloved husband,

And in the world of politics - a legend in his times.

The man is gone! But his memory lives…

An inspiration now, and every coming day

To his beloved country-and the free world.

Now, with God's blessings, he will rest in peace!

Queen Elizabeth II

Heir to the throne of the British Empire,

Queen Elizabeth strides thru decades of war,

turmoil, and struggle for political power,

Social unrest and remnants of the postwar.

She comes through chaos and challenging times

Facing a growing- furiously changing world-

But the Monarch remains undaunted and alive,

As her courage and wisdom are put to the test.

Gallantly poised over domestic and external events

She stands firm in the defense of her royal ancestry-

A true leader who commands admiration and respect.

May the Lord bless-and long live- Her Royal Majesty!

Lady Di

Lady in a land of power she was born,

The Queen of Hearts who drove thru life

Daring into worlds where lives are torn

By misery and despair, as they try to survive.

Lady Di dealt with people of different trades,

But shunned from prejudice that binds.

She was a caring princess, strong and brave,

Who raised her voice on behalf of Mankind.

More than a noble figure of the throne

She was a blazing spirit of this world,

Delivering the seeds of human hope

To the suffering souls that never rest!

Martin Luther King, Jr.

(Free Man)

To step out from servitude that binds and dulls,

Or worse, from slavery that handicaps the mind,

Takes a man of great courage, daring and guts,

And calls for a freedom desire that can't be denied.

Good men had been fighting from slavery times,

Then, Luther King Jr. would follow their steps,

Struggling and fighting for his people's rights.

Martin, a man who never quit - until his final day.

He learned from early childhood to love our God,

And cherished the principles of human rights:

That all men are equal in the eyes of the Lord,

Regardless of the prejudice of humankind!

Einstein

The great mathematician pierced trough knowledge

Probing the elusive universe of Science,

Blending his mind with those we acknowledge

Set free mankind from tribal life and ignorance.

Looking to unfold the mysteries of time and space

Einstein developed theories that shed new light

Over a complex, ever-growing, scientific universe,

Driven by formulae and the intellectual mind.

However, beside his Science and wild imagination,

We find an interesting and emphatic human side,

For the scientist's passion for the wonders of Creation

Echoed his passion for the defense of human rights.

Freud

The creator and master of the Psychoanalysis-
His tool designed to explore the unconscious mind-
Endeavored to decipher, under his analyses,
The dreams and nightmares of the mind of man.

Freud delved into the fantasies of humankind
Lying at the core of the subconscious world,
Figments that turn to chaos people's lives,
Leaving no peace, no sanity, no mental rest.

With great passion he came through his times
Ignoring prejudice and orthodox rejections-
Even physical pain the last years of his life-
To bring his work to universal recognition.

Davinci

Davinci, a prodigy of the human race,

Delivers forbidden knowledge from his time,

Merging reluctant feelings of a sleeping world

With his remarkable ideas of the universal man.

As enigmatic as his Mona Lisa smile,

Leonardo leaps through centuries of darkness

fascinating with his designs the human mind,

Then, at the mercy of unthinkable madness.

Rising beyond the labyrinths of Middle Age

He storms through radicals and partisans,

And soars above the barriers of the ancient sage

To becoming the quintessence of Renaissance.

Michelangelo

Towering above past and contemporary geniuses

And setting the patterns for next generations,

The sculptor, painter, and reluctant architect,

Amazed the world with his master creations.

In the chiseling world of beauty and power

He molded marble into seemingly living human beings;

His craft divinely guided by his drive and the desire

To carve in stone his feelings and his dreams.

Stubborn and passionate Michelangelo painted,

Defying the motives that spurred his sensibility;

And as his tormented body and mind were tested,

His monumental craft rose him to immortality.

Shakespeare

With a verb full of wisdom and a sense of tragedy,
Shakespeare pictured a world of fantasy and reality
In his superb collection of characters and mystery
That rose beyond medieval times into modernity.

From misfortune of love, and sacrifice and death,
To kings, and witches and their magic spells;
He portrayed ruthless personalities like Macbeth,
As well as Romeo and Juliette's tragic tale.

Through his skillful, dramatic characterization,
William's perceptive and resourceful mind
Exposed fairly people's concerns and situations
Harmonizing with his enigmatic world and times.

Voltaire

Deep and incisive, his sharpened word
Cut through the frailties of society
To expose and ridicule a hollow world
Ruled by nobility and bureaucracy.

Voltaire's shrewd, sarcastic, moody mind,
Slashed with the passion of a killing bird,
Defying the ruling powers of his time
With the sword of his merciless verb.

Banished, imprisoned, beaten and betrayed,
The literary genius who's fame and reputation
For fighting for justice-at all costs- became
A top leader in the Golden Age of Illustration.

Elvis Presley

(King of Rock)

Rocking the world he led his life,

Singing the music people loved,

And like a shooting star soaring the sky

He became the undisputed King of Rock.

"The King," they called him, decades past,

For his unique, melodious, thrilling voice,

And his unusual "rocking style"

Swarming their hearts and minds with joy.

Elvis, the unforgettable soul of Rock and Roll,

Came through his glorious, roaring times,

Leaving mankind a singing, happy note,

And the scent of a candid super star.

David Bowie

(Rock Star)

From British lands he came to join the stars

Of an emerging world of Rock and Roll,

And captured legions in his gleaming craft

Setting dramatic patterns of his own.

He came to America to share his art

And let his music tour the world of rock;

He came to spark the feelings of his fans

With his peculiar way rock people loved.

Bowie remains a legend to these days

Who came thru many changes in his life,

And after being exalted to the Hall of Fame,

Death stopped the rhythms of his heart.

Pope John Paul II

(Spiritual Traveler)

The Adamant traveler of the spiritual world

Who grasped the essence of the human mind

And faced from childhood the social unrest-

For him, the bells are ringing over humankind.

He came across the boundaries of man

Spreading the seeds of Love and Peace;

A leading messenger of God's Design

In a temporal quest over human beliefs.

And as he steps beyond his mortal bonds

His memory is a brief reflection to mankind

Illuminating the path to the House of the Lord,

Where we will meet at the end of our time.

Mackenzie Scott

(Golden Heart)

Soaring far beyond her wealthy elite,

A compassionate soul, a Golden Heart,

Steps in the middle of the catastrophe

To lend a pious hand as best she can.

One of a kind- a modern warrior-

Mackenzie strides through life

Undaunted, challenging the odds

With fortitude, and a persuasive smile.

Mindful of the pandemic threat to mankind,

The young crusader- diligent, steadfast-

Strikes with the power of a magic wand

To alleviate the suffering of million hearts!

Columbus

Daring into the mysteries of undiscovered seas,
Driven by his imagination, grit and faith,
The boldest navigator people would ever see
Brought ancient civilizations to a new world.

His legendary Caravels sailed thru the mist
Beyond the limits of man's superstition,
To find an ocean route to the Far East…
But found a land to challenge his ambition.

Centuries past beyond the Seaman's dreams
To the modern complexities of humankind,
There are still mysteries beyond our streams,
Waiting for another Christopher to find…

Nostradamus

Reaching beyond his times into future events,

The skillful master described his prophesies

In obscure, concealed ways in his quatrains,

For the man of tomorrow- the judge of his beliefs.

Nostradamus, as well as Newton, Mozart, Brahms,

Copernicus, Galileo, Davinci, and Albert Einstein,

Provide undeniable proof that the mind of man,

In-spite of man- is the ultimate wonder of mankind.

And him-a controversial Oracle of Human Fate -

A magician? A genius? A man of God? -

Still puzzles humanity with his riddles of yesterday.

But how did he foresee his visions? We'll never know.

Julius Caesar

Victorious he marched against the enemies of Rome

Suppressing the uprisings of barbaric tribes,

Destroying the threats to his imperial home,

To maintain order and protect his homeland.

After so many wars he faced a turning point in life,

So he marched against Rome thru the forbidden path;

And leading his army onto the city grounds he attacked,

Overthrowing the government of the Republic overnight.

Then, Caesar took the Republic under his command;

But plotting and treason never abandon power,

And he was betrayed and murdered by the hand

Of senators afraid of - and opposed - to his empire!

Hannibal

Thundering trough the forests leading to the empire

The Sicilian commander marched against Rome

Crushing the Roman legions in his rapid-fire,

By Implementing amazing tactics of his own.

The coming days turned into years of agony,

As Hannibal's warfare strategies faded in time,

And every battle won turned into a Pyrrhic victory,

Leaving a shrinking army fighting for their lives.

Zama became the Carthaginian's final battle,

As the last hope for reinforcements from home

Was harshly cut by the Roman commander,

Ending Hannibal's shocking threat to Rome.

TEACHER

From the very beginnings of civilization
To present day–in a never-ending quest-
The Teacher paves the way, thru education,
For us to conquer ignorance and keep abreast.

Teachers are great performers,
Passionate and devoted to the human race,
Nurturing students minds with knowledge,
Leading the way to make a better world

They are devoted laborers of our minds,
Helping to improve our means to move ahead
And providing for us a better way of life.
Let's honor them- as they deserve!

Politician

Bold and assertive, pleasant but domineering,
The charismatic, overwhelming man,
Cuts through the mob to take the lead
And seize control over his fellowman.

Since his beginnings, far back in time,
He has taken control over this land,
Whether as chieftain of the troglodytes
Or chief commander of the modern man.

The politician, as leader of the human race,
Plays an extremely, most important part;
So he must wisely deal the crises he will face,
For in his hands he holds the destiny of Mankind!

Writer

Collector of ideas and events of Nature and Mankind,

Or creator of worlds of fantasy, romance and fiction,

He brings his feelings to enliven people's minds,

To awaken their spirit and enlighten their wisdom.

His craft, bold and defiant, travels through time

Unveiling secrets, knowledge, works, and dreams

Of human beings whose remarkable lives

Contribute to man's survival and well-being.

Moved by the deepest feelings of his heart

The writer tracks the essence of the human-race

To write about historic treasures of the past,

Or share his vision of man beyond this world.

Spartans

Set against the unconquerable forces of destiny

The greatest warriors of immortal Greece

came through the passages of human history

to inspire future generations with their deed.

Three Hundred Spartans turned into a human wall

Facing the largest army of ancient times,

To block the pathway to the Persian hordes

With every single beat of their courageous lives.

With broken spears, but rock-solid hearts,

They battled through long hours, day by day,

Trading their blood for freedom, as they charged,

Fighting - like the killing machines they were.

Commanded by Leonidas, their fearless king,

The legendary warriors fought without rest,

For there would be no mercy for these human beings

who made Thermopylae their final quest.

Gladiator

Demanding sweat and blood from every battle,

Anguish, despair, broken flesh and bones,

The Imperial Circus welcomes every fighter

To the torturing challenges of ancient Rome.

The furious charge of unstoppable chariots

Blends with the flashing swords of burning steel,

As the roar of the crowd compels the warriors

And their merciless thumbs drop for the kill.

Only the fittest live through many encounters

Until they face a greater gladiator

That cuts them loose from mortal bondage

And sends them to the Arena of the Creator.

Veteran

You fought away from home, in foreign lands,

Against your country's enemies, and more…

Your life at stake, you kept on going thru the war,

Sworn to defend your nation under an alien sky.

To recall those events is a nightmare:

The fallen friends, the bloodshed either way,

The loneliness and the resentment - who would care?

And the burning desire to be home - so far away…

And now you are back! The fight is over!

But there's a broken heart, a troubled mind;

And from the memories of war you won't recover.

Oh Lord! Will there ever be peace in humankind?

Cop

Pledged against the elements of crime,

He never stops his march around the clock

To uphold the law, protect innocent lives,

And, as best as he can- to do his job.

Cop roams around the city, day and night,

His life in jeopardy, at every turning point,

As he patrols under the city lights

And strolls through the forbidden joints.

Daring he comes along the unsteady path

Facing all enemies from the dark side,

From the top-notch glamour to the sinister dive,

To protect citizens and safeguard human lives.

Narcissus

He stared into the quiet waters of the lake

At the spellbinding image of his manhood.

And fell in love with the reflection of himself

Unable to withstand his powerful, magnetic looks.

Narcissus became a prisoner of his reflection-

The punishment for his conceited, arrogant behavior.

One day, unable to withdraw from his own fascination,

He plunged into the waters, to end his cruel obsession.

Narcissus mythological character is still alive,

Wandering through the forests of the imagination,

Hunting the elusive image in his mind,

Forever trapped in his self-contemplation.

www.ingramcontent.com/pod-product-compliance
Lightning Source LLC
Chambersburg PA
CBHW072142150726
48002CB00004B/1590